Love, Marianna
Dani, Elly and
Nadia

We
love you!

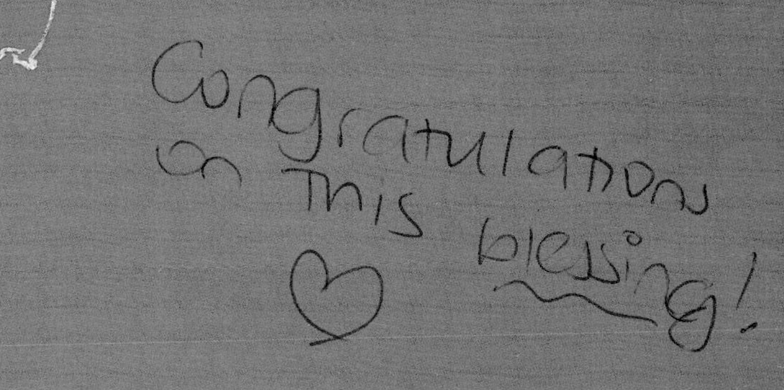

Adapted by Jean-Baptiste Baronian

Typeset in Weiss.
Text design by Madeleine Budnick and Amy Nathan.

Printed in Singapore.

Library of Congress Catalog Card #97-32208
ISBN: 0-8118-2031-9

Distributed in Canada by Raincoast Books
9050 Shaughnessy Street
Vancouver, British Columbia V6P 6E5

10 9 8 7 6 5

Chronicle Books LLC
85 Second Street
San Francisco, California 94105
www.chroniclebooks.com/Kids

I Love You with All My Heart

by Noris Kern

chronicle books · san francisco

One brisk morning, Polo ambled down to the shore to fish. While he was in the water his friend Walter came along.

"Polo, the water is cold. Be careful not to get sick or you will worry your mother who loves you with all her heart," Walter said.

Polo was curious. What did Walter mean?

"How can my mother love me with all her heart?" Polo wondered.

He decided to find out. He splashed out of his fishing hole and headed home.

On his way, Polo met his friend Pinpin. "Pinpin, how does your mother love you?" asked Polo.

Pinpin thought for a moment.

"My mother loves me with all her wings," he said. Then he picked up a snowball and cuddled it under his wings. "Like this!" he said.

"Hmm," thought Polo. "My mother doesn't love me with wings." So Polo continued on his way. Soon he met Felix.

"Felix, how does your mother love you?" asked Polo.

"She loves me with all her flippers," Felix replied.

Felix picked up Pinpin and
gave him a big flippery squeeze.

"Hmm," thought Polo. "My mother doesn't love me with flippers." So Polo continued on his way. Soon Jessie bounded up. "Jessie," Polo asked, "How does your mother love you?"

Jessie was surprised. "What a funny question. My mother loves me with all her teeth," replied Jessie.

Then he gave Polo a playful nibble.

Polo giggled, "My mother doesn't love me with teeth."

So Pinpin, Felix, and Jessie all set out to find Polo's mother.

When Polo saw his mother, he crawled on her back and snuggled against her warm fur.

"Your fur is soft," he said to his mother. "Does that mean that you love me with all your fur?"

"Yes, I love you with all my fur," she replied. "But that's not all."

"I love you with
my eyes that shine
when I see you."

"I love you with my nose because you smell so sweet.

I love you with my mouth when I kiss kiss kiss you."

"I love you with my paws when I tickle you and lift you in the air above me.

I love you with my back when you ride upon it. And, I love you with my belly when you hug me tight."

"Polo, I love you with all my heart," she said.

Polo gave his mother a big hug. It had been a long day, and he was ready to crawl into bed.

"You know, I love you with all my heart, too," said Polo. And he curled up to his mother and fell fast asleep.